THE BOOKSTORE GHOST

by **Barbara Maitland**
pictures by **Nadine Bernard Westcott**

DUTTON CHILDREN'S BOOKS
New York

For Nick—B. M.

For Becky—N. W.

Text copyright © 1998 by Barbara Maitland
Illustrations copyright © 1998 by Nadine Bernard Westcott

CIP Data is available.

Published in the United States 1998 by Dutton Children's Books,
a member of Penguin Putnam Inc.
375 Hudson Street, New York, New York 10014

Printed in Hong Kong

First Edition

3 5 7 9 10 8 6 4 2

ISBN 0-525-46049-7

Chapter One

Mr. Brown liked three things:

ghost books, cheese, and cats.

"I will buy a bookstore,"

said Mr. Brown.

And he did!

He sold only ghost books.

4

Then he said, "I need a friend.

I will get a cat."

And he did!

His cat was not like other cats.

She did not like fish.

But she loved cheese.

Mr. Brown and his cat ate cheese

for breakfast, lunch, and dinner.

They lived above the bookstore.

Mice lived in their house, too.

Chapter Two

One day, a woman came in to buy a book.

She saw a mouse.

"Eeeek!" she screamed.

She ran out of the store.

A man ran out, too.

"The Black Cat Bookstore

has mice," they said.

Nobody wanted to come to the store.

"This is your job," Mr. Brown told his cat.

"You are the cat. You catch the mice."

So the cat went to the mouse hole.

The mice were scared.

But the cat said,

"I am not like other cats. I like mice."

And she did!

The cat and the mice played together.

Mr. Brown was not happy.

"Those mice are scaring people away!"

he said.

"If they do not come in to buy my books,

I will have to close the store down.

You have three days to catch the mice,"

he told his cat.

"Tomorrow is

Day One."

"Mr. Brown says you are scaring the people

away," the cat said to the mice.

"But this is a *ghost* bookstore,"

said a mouse. "It *should* be scary."

Then the cat said, "I have a plan."

Chapter Three

Day One came.

Day One for the cat and Day One of the plan.

A boy was walking by the store.

CRASH!

A book fell off a shelf.

THUMP!

Another book fell on the floor.

"Did you see that?" said the boy.

He went into the store.

CRASH! THUMP!

More books fell.

"The Black Cat Bookstore

has a real ghost," the boy said.

Then his friends came into the store.

Day Two came.

Day Two for the cat

and Day Two of the plan.

The ghost was very busy.

So was the store.

Everyone wanted to see the ghost.

The cat purred.

Her plan was working.

PURRR...

On Day Three, the store was

busier than ever.

At the end of the day,

there was only one book left!

"I will not have to close the store down

after all," said Mr. Brown to his cat.

"Tonight, we will celebrate.

We will have a cheese feast."

Chapter Four

"I like my ghost," said Mr. Brown.

"But I still don't like those mice.

Have you caught them?"

The cat purred.

She rubbed against Mr. Brown's legs.

Then she walked away.

"Shall I follow you?" he asked.

He followed her to a bookshelf.

"Maybe I will see my ghost,"

he said.

The mice waited for him.

They pushed the last book off the shelf.

CRASH!

The mice looked at Mr. Brown.

Mr. Brown looked at the mice.

"I see," said Mr. Brown.

"Do ghosts like cheese?"

he asked the mice.

Now they all live together.

The store is always busy.

And Mr. Brown likes four things:

ghost books, cheese, his cat . . .

and his ghost!